LED BY AN EAGLE

OMAR BLUE SAGA

BOOK TWO

By O. Warfield

Omar Blue

How could I not write about him.

Strong, loyal and beautiful.

The friend I hoped he would be.

Dedicated to my loving husband and daughter.

I could not have done this without you.

THE MOUNTAIN LION'S MISTAKE

(Chapter One)

Was a sunny day

Big things on the way

At K-9 Town, USA.

Rottweiler Brady

And Pitbull Sammy

Enjoying the month of May.

They were on their way

Back to the pack

To tell leader Omar Blue.

They'd just been accosted

By mountain lions

And what they had to do.

They met up with Omar

Headed their way

He asked, "What are you two up to?"

Pitbull Sammy

Was glad to speak

"We were coming to find you.

We met some mountain lions back there

One even threw a threat

He teed Professor Brady off

Don't think he's got up yet."

(*Rottweiler Brady*)

"I'm Professor Brady only to the pack

Outside I'm Rottweiler Brady

Ain't like he didn't know my name

And said teaching was for a lady.

I taught him quick

How a teacher teaches

Mountain lions too.

Then we figured in case

 They're hunting trouble

We'd better come tell you.

The mountain lions are starting up

Don't think they like us here

May as well bring it to a head

Make sure they have it clear.

Was the lion Booby

Leading them

A total of only three.

Who would have thought

They'd have the nerve

To confront this Pit and me.

Then Pitbull Sammy took his turn

A big smile on his face

"I was hoping they all would join in

But the others kept their place.

I agree with Brady, something is up

We think they had it planned

But they didn't guess the consequence

Of calling the professor's hand."

Omar looked at both of them

Proud to have them in his pack

"We'll alert the rest of the elders

And hope those cats come back.

In the meantime

Get them out of your heads

There's other things to do

We're taking a trip, to see my kin

I want them all to meet you.

We're all a little restless

It's time for the puppies' first run

It will do us all, a bit of good

And we'll have a lot of fun."

PUPPY TALK

(Chapter 2)

K-9 Town was buzzing

They were visiting Omar Blue's kin

The females were getting things ready

The puppies were in the den.

The other puppies were silent

Listening to Lee, Lii and Luu

Tell how Professor Brady

Broke the giant mountain lion in two.

The Chihuahua puppy triplets

Were the puppy leaders too

Said that lion should have come to them

To hear what their professor could do.

They laughed until their tummies ached
Then they laughed some more
"Bet we could handle that mountain lion
If he bangs on our door."

Or maybe we'll get to see him
On the way to Leader Omar's kin
We'll run away from the Shepherds
And beat him up again."

Poodle Sophie Jean came in
Schoolmarm and Brady's wife
She had to hold her laugher in
It might just save a life.

"What's this you say about running away
While the Shepherds are watching you
I tell you now if you try it
We'll be all over you.

Not talking about the professor
Not talking about the Shepherds too
Cause me and the female elders
Are the ones who'll handle you.

Now quiet down, and take a nap
There's a long, long trip ahead
When you wake up we'll be leaving
But remember what I just said."

The puppies heard every word she said

And knew each one was true

The female elders didn't play

When they came after you.

They'd wait awhile, until they got big

That lion would still be there

They'd take the professor with them

Then the females wouldn't care.

So off they went to dreamland

Nothing else they could do

In a few days they'd be bigger

They'd take Pitbull Sammy too.

FORCES TO RECKON WITH

(Chapter 3)

Over under the Big Oak Tree

Two forces had just met

Komondor Rasta Mama, and Great Dane Granny

As friendly as they could get.

Komondor Mama was speaking

"I've heard so much about you

It's said you cast away evil

Which is something I can't do.

My gift says trouble's over us

Just what I've yet to see

I think we should join together

And not work separately."

Great Dane Granny, looked at her
"How awesome we will be
You with your gift of second site
To help ward off the enemy.

Let's call ourselves the Seers
The pack will like it fine
They'll know we're helping Omar
Using your gift and using mine.

We'll travel together, all the way
You tell me what you see
Then I'll cast away the bad spirits
How safe our pack will be.

Now let's go tell leader Omar Blue

He'll be so glad to hear

That we'll be watching, over our pack

Over those he holds so dear."

Just then Omar Blue came up

Somehow he'd heard it all

He smiled to himself, then said out loud

"Stop worrying, have a ball.

I know the trouble you're gonna see

But believe me all is fine

And when you both see what it is

Remember this trouble is mine.

I want you both to enjoy this trip

So I tell you what I'll do

I'll keep in mind your special gifts

And stay in touch with you".

The newly named Seers both spoke to him

"Omar Blue we know you well

When something happens with your pack

You act and then you tell.

So we'll just keep an eye on you

Have a ball just like you say

But when the spirits speak to us

We'll be coming fast your way."

GETTING READY

(Chapter 4)

On the other side of the Big Oak Tree

Rhodesian Ridgebacks Koffee and Tee

Talking to Bulldogs Betty and Jim

About how they must depart.

They had to go after the mountain lions

To keep the threat away from the pack

The four would take the lead right now

Before the journey's start.

Was then that Omar Blue appeared

He knew they had to go

Hunting lions was in their blood

Never thought of saying no.

He said, "You four, you go ahead
But do what I tell you to
Don't approach the mountain lions
Just keep them in your view.

They're not enough to be a threat
Though they'll plan to pick up more
Let them see us leaving
They'll follow us for sure.

The four looked at each other
Then back at Omar Blue
They saw a plan was in the works
What was their leader up to?

They'd do just what he told them

They'd look but wouldn't touch

Cause Omar's plans were special

The canines knew that much.

So Koffee and Tee

Betty and Jim

Ran off to take the lead

The Ridgebacks and the Bulldogs

A striking sight indeed.

MOUNTAIN LION STRATEGY

(Chapter 5)

When Mountain Lion Booby got up

He was mad as he could be

He told his lion buddies

"We'll get that pack, you'll see.

Looks like they're going somewhere

We won't let them get away

They won't expect us to follow

Then pounce on them one day.

We've got kin any way they go

We'll pick them up as we pass

Omar's pack won't know what hit them

We'll be rid of them at last.

Go get word to our kin folk
Let them know we're coming their way
Gonna teach those dogs, a thing or two
Make them glad to go away."

Booby's friends were thoughtful
They knew of Omar's pack
They led a peaceful lifestyle
But could stand up to any attack.

The mountain lions weren't the first
To want them to go away
But here they stayed, never afraid
Looking forward to each new day.

Omar's pack without him
Was the meanest ever seen
Putting Omar Blue back in the mix
Gave a new meaning to mean.

Then add on that big crazy wolf
They call him Bennie Ba
He's now a member of Omar's Pack
Maybe we should stay away.

We'll go and tell the kin folk
See what they have to say
But then we might be better off
Heading the other way.

OFF TO SEE OMAR'S KIN

(Chapter 6)

They were leaving their beloved town
A thing so hard to do
But all was well and they'd be back
They were following Omar Blue.

When the elders and the puppies
Left K-9 Town that day
They were heading for new adventures
That would surely come their way.

While the elder males were walking
Deciding which way they'd go
The females followed close behind

The puppies now in tow.

As Omar Blue was moving out
He happened to glance up high
Where a beautiful giant eagle
Was slowly passing by.

It circled Omar Blue's whole pack
Though way up in the sky
Then flew off like a flash of light
Without catching another eye.

They'd move all day and rest all night
No reason to travel fast
They'd enjoy this time away from home
To meet Omar's kin at last.

They gave little thought

To the mountain lions

But of course they'd be aware

If the lions tried to spoil their trip

What they got would be quite rare.

So on they went the first day

Until night began to fall

They stopped to eat

Get off their feet

And now they'd have a ball.

They gathered in a circle

Elder males and females too

The puppies over to the side

But always in full view.

The pack had so much fun that night

They didn't get much rest

Couldn't tell it the next morning though

They all were at their best.

The females decided they needed a run

The puppies hurried into sacks

They'd waited for this time to come

Loved riding the female's backs.

The males gathered to see them

Found a spot up in the hills

Watching the females run like this

Was among their greatest thrills.

They started rather slowly

But soon picked up speed

The smallest having as much fun

As the big dogs in the lead.

The males were all so happy

As proud as they could be

Then Omar Blue stood up and said,

"Do you all see what I see?"

It was the Komondor Rasta Mama

And Great Dane Granny too

Prancing through the young females

Then gone from everyone's view.

The males couldn't contain it

Even leader Omar Blue

They laughed, howled and jumped up high
Knowing what they saw was true.

They knew the feisty "Seers"
Had been mixing potions again
So this was just another feat
Wonder which one would win.

Then Omar looked at Major Diggs
He knew he'd seen it too
The looks on those two faces
As they were passing through.

They were on a mission, that's for sure
Wonder what they planned to do
Better go behind them just in case

Major Diggs would watch the crew.

CHASING THE SPIRITS

(Chapter 7)

Omar took off like a shot

He ran at his top speed

Then slowed up when he saw them

Didn't want to take the lead.

He knew now where they were going

Gonna check on the scouting four

The ridgebacks and the bulldogs

In their dreams the ones they saw.

Meanwhile watching the mountain lions

Doing what they had been told

Koffee, Tee, Betty and Jim

Hearing Booby talking bold.

They noticed everything he said
Omar Blue had said it too
But they would never understand
How he knew what those lions would do.

Though they listened for awhile
They played and had much fun
Especially bulldogs Betty and Jim
Whose romance had just begun.

Then suddenly their ears perked up
Each one had heard the sound
They turned and looked across the way
Surprised at what they found.

It was the Komondor Rasta Mama

And Great Dane Granny too

Coming at them mighty fast

Calling, "We just had to see you!"

The scouts knew of the potions

So they cast the feat aside

More important now, was them being there

How'd they know where they would hide.

Was Great Dane Granny talking now

"We had to come find you

There's danger lurking around the pack

So this we had to do.

We ran away the bad spirits

Surrounding our mighty pack

Then had to do the same for you

Now we have to run right back.

Soon Omar will be looking

To see where we have gone

Don't want our leader to worry

We'd better keep moving on."

Then Rasta Mama said to them

"She's right we'd better go

We'll slip back in among our kin

Omar Blue will never know."

(They both laughed out loud)

Omar just sat and listened

While the Seers had their say

They'd done what they felt they had to

Had to do it their own way.

Great Dane Granny

  And Rasta Mama

Those two were having fun

No need to even mention

The danger in what they'd done.

THE SEERS REPENT

(Chapter 8)

Later on that afternoon

The pair came heads hung low

Potions wearing off now

Tired and walking slow.

"Leader Omar we have to tell you

We did something bad today

We left the pack, went on our own

We ran a long, long way.

They told about their visit

To the others in his care

We had to chase the bad spirits

We knew were hanging there.

So don't you worry Omar
Our scouts are now okay
Doing just what you told them
And taking time to play.

Now please excuse us Leader
We're as tired as can be."
They turned and said to each other
"Let's go try some of that tea!"

Omar Blue looked after them
The two were quite a pair
They'd take a bit of watching
He'd make the others aware.

The Seers also didn't know

He'd signaled his scouting four

As they were leaving to follow them

Omar Blue was what they saw.

They understood their leader

Without a spoken word

They knew the Seers would be safe

With Omar riding herd.

Now back to Booby and his pride

He'd added twenty-two

But still didn't think that was enough

To handle Omar Blue.

"They're headed up into the hills

We got plenty kin up there
Let's wait a little longer
Then we'll start to prepare.

Gonna teach them not to mess with us
Gonna make them leave their land
When we get finished with Omar's Pack
They'll finally understand.

As Mountain Lion Booby got on his way
He glanced into the sky
Where the ugliest eagle he'd ever seen
Was slowly passing by.

It circled the mountain lion pride
Too low but still in the sky

Then flew off like a flash of light

After catching each lion's eye.

THE PUPPIES CLUBHOUSE

(Chapter 9)

Back again to the puppy pack

What are those puppies up to

They are being mighty quiet now

Keeping something in full view.

"It's beautiful," said Cocker puppy Joe

And the other puppies agreed

"It will make a wonderful clubhouse

It's exactly what we need."

Cooley Junior the Komondor, spoke up next

"We're here for a whole day

We'll fix our clubhouse up real nice

And have a good place to play.

We'll get furs from my Pa Pa
To make our beds tonight
The elders will let us stay here
As long as we're in sight."

"That's right" said Maggie the Beagle puppy
"We'll be all on our own
We're gonna have lots of fun tonight
If they let us stay alone."

Was Poodle Dumplin's turn to speak
"Let's gather what we need."
They all ran out together
Each trying to take the lead.

Of course their leader heard all this
No need to ask just how
Omar loved overseeing the puppies
Especially times like now.

They were always planning something new
Always busy having fun
That's just the way he wanted it
Their lives had just begun.

Soon enough through teaching
They'd have to face this land
Strong, proud, and fearless
With the rest of his pack they'd stand.

The puppies had gathered

Their odds and ends

To make their clubhouse great

The elders weren't allowed in there

At the door they'd have to wait.

As day went on, dusk came along

They went and joined the pack

They ate then told the elders

"We're leaving but we'll be back."

They noticed not an elder budged

Acted like they didn't care

Couldn't they see they were leaving

For their clubhouse waaay over there.

The puppies walked off slowly

It was getting pretty dark

They could hardly see their clubhouse now

Should have left some kind of mark.

They made it to the front door

But didn't rush to go in

By now they were pretty tired

Wanting home and their "real" den.

The clubhouse was looking different now

Kind of spooky one might say

How could it look like this now

It was beautiful all day!

They looked around at each other

What were they going to do

They didn't want to go in there

Then they heard Omar Blue.

"So this is the place you talked about

We weren't to come in here

That's right this is your Clubhouse

I'll go to sleep elsewhere".

"No, no leader Omar!!!

We're not gonna make a fuss

You're tired and you need your rest

So come lay down with us."

Omar smiling to himself

Said "How very nice of you

If it weren't for your kindness

I don't know what I'd do."

The puppies smiled at their leader

Then they jumped for joy

No longer feeling tired

What a leader, boy oh boy!

Omar sat and watched them

Until their strength was gone

One by one they came to him

For an empty spot to lie on.

He had told the other elders

About his evening plans

So they could get in on it too

A Pack of puppy fans.

In the morning when the pups woke up

Omar Blue had already gone

Their clubhouse was looking pretty again

What do you think went wrong?

DOING WHAT BEE BEE DOES BEST

(Chapter 10)

Omar was with Afghan Bee Bee

They both were taking a break

Him from being Leader

Her from using the rake.

The rake was a process that she used

On the female elder's hair

The ones who'd never been before

Under her fancy care.

Today it would be Mistie

Sandy's mate the St. Bernard

Bee Bee had big plans for her

But it was gonna be hard.

She loved her place within the pack
She couldn't ask for more
She made the females feel special
That's what they came to her for.

And when they left, they'd strut around
For all the pack to see.
Just one more thing, to make Omar's Pack
The best that it could be.

She treasured her time with Omar Blue
She thought he liked it too
But no one could read their leader
Just something they couldn't do.

Maybe at the journey's end
When they all have met his kin
They'd get a better understanding
Of their leader then.

When Bee Bee got to the females
Mistie was already there
The other females had started
Raking out her hair.

"We couldn't wait, we had to try
What you've taught us to do
Her hair is looking pretty neat
But the rest is up to you."

Bee Bee looked at all her friends

Loved having them around

They'd welcomed her, the very first day

What a wonderful pack she'd found.

"Okay you all come gather around

See what I'm gonna do

Cause when we finish

With Mistie's hair

She'll be beautiful just like you."

Bee Bee then went right to work

Doing what she did so well

While the females sat and watched her

As if under her spell.

She finally finished Mistie's hair

It took a while to do

Then Mistie sat back astonished

"Bee Bee I do thank you!"

The other females went closer

They all pretended to fuss

"Bee Bee you gotta do ours again

Cause Mistie looks better than us."

(They all laughed out loud)

"I'd start right now, but you've forgot

The promise that we made

To Lab Retrievers Jai & Ach

They're waiting for our aid."

A MEAL TO REMEMBER

(Chapter 11)

Jai and Ach could prepare a meal

Like no other K-9s there

They loved to feed the hungry bunch

And did it with much care.

They'd send the pack to gather food

The males would bring back fish

The females brought all sorts of things

To make a tasty dish.

Then Jai and Ach would get to work

No help was needed then

They'd set out a delicious meal

And call the whole pack in.

The puppies were a different story
They were never far away
While Jai and Ach would fuss at them
They'd give them treats all day.

They had a puppy in the mix
Puppy Piper was her name
She too had fun, waiting for the treats
She was proud to play the game.

Getting back to the females
They'd gone to handle their chore
The fun they were having, on this trip
They'd never had before.

That night when all sat down to eat
Jai and Ach sat with them too
They loved to watch the pack at work
Eating their K-9 stew.

Then sure enough, after the meal
They'd stay and talk awhile
Then thank the two for another fine meal
All leaving wearing a smile.

Omar was the last to leave
 "I want to thank you two
I like the way you treat the pack
They sure are fond of you.

The time we spent together here

Meant more than you could know

Again we reinforced our bond

Thanks for making it so."

Jai and Ach beamed with joy

Their leader talking like this

They loved the pack

And would never go back

To a life they didn't miss.

They liked preparing these hearty meals

And ordering the pack around

They'd threaten not to feed them

If anyone made a sound.

They followed every order

It was all a part of the game

They knew Jai and Ach would feed them

But they'd listen just the same.

Omar had called his scouts in

He wanted them with the pack

Supper gave him a reason

But he wouldn't let them go back.

The mountain lions were gathering kin

They'd tripled their numbers too

But the plans they made to hurt his pack

They still had time to undo.

None of them were worried

That's not the way they'd live

They'd handle the trouble when it came

Giving all they had to give.

BOOBY'S PLAN

(Chapter 12)

Mountain Lion Booby was filled with joy

He thought he had a plan

But why spend any time on that

They'd catch them as they ran.

Booby wasn't very smart

But he should have noticed too

The higher they went into the hills

The smaller their numbers grew.

There was no explanation

For the others didn't know

By then their numbers were so large

Who cared, let um go.

The only thing he asked his Pride
And he was speaking mighty low
"Save that Rottweiler Brady for me
Gonna beat him nice and slow.

Should have seen the way he snuck me
I didn't fall, I slipped
Just so happens I hit my head
Made it look like I'd been clipped."

The others had heard the story
Quite different from what he said
If the Rottweiler was that easy
Booby would have taken his head.

They were far up in the hills now

A place they'd never been

It seemed so dark and desolate

Though the sun was shining in.

There was something wrong about this place

They all felt this was true

But what it was, they didn't know

Didn't even have a clue.

The Pride went to talk to Booby

"We've waited long enough

Tonight we're gonna show them

Omar's Pack don't look that tough."

Meanwhile down below the hill

Omar Blue sat with his pack
He could feel the tension rising
Why don't we start the attack!

They gathered in a circle
Each knowing what to do
A tougher pack you'll never see
Led by Omar Blue.

Bennie Ba the big white wolf
Walked over to Omar's side
Big dogs, Brady, Sammy, Kooley and Jim
Made the front line seem quite wide.

The others were behind them
Too numerous to call

Shepherds, Ridgebacks, Pitbulls, Hounds

No way to name them all.

It was Paco the angry Chihuahua

Who yelled out from the back

"Let's get those mountain lions

We'll teach them to follow our Pack!"

Somehow the whole pack heard him

And they rallied to the sound

Gonna take the fight to the lions

No way to settle down.

Omar yelled "LET'S DO IT!"

With a deadly look on his face

"And don't worry any one of you

Cause we all gonna leave this place."

The females gathered the puppies
Who did what they were taught to do
 Brady and Sophie had trained them well
To stay out of the enemies view.

The females would protect them
Their number one thing to do
But the elder Seers spoke up then
"We'll protect them, you go too."

The females looked suspiciously
It was Great Dane Jennie who spoke
"Grandma what have you two done
You know this ain't no joke."

"Jennie don't you sass me

And Rasta Mama here

We made a special potion

When we knew the battle was near.

Together we're stronger than 20 of you

We'll keep our pups real calm

If the mountain lions make it over here

We'll inflict plenty harm."

Rasta Mama spoke up then

"I'll prove what we can do"

She ran and kicked a big tree

Her foot went right through.

The females looked at each other

The Seers had done it again

They'd protect the pups no matter what

They'd be with them until the end.

They ran to their male elders

They left the Seers behind

Not worried about the puppies now

They knew they'd be just fine.

THE MOUNTAIN LIONS' DOUBT

(Chapter 13)

Meanwhile at the top of the hill

Booby's pride was looking down

Thinking maybe this wouldn't work

Their numbers weren't that sound.

The dogs were outnumbered three to one

They knew but didn't care

They completely turned the attack around

Only Omar's Pack would dare.

We'll do what we came here for

Gonna wipe out Omar's Pack

But when we leave this mysterious place

We don't ever wanna come back.

The mountain lions headed down the hill

Gonna meet them face to face

Each had an eerie feeling

There was something about this place.

As they went further down the hill

Omar's pack was coming up

They were about to meet in the middle

When something else came...

OMARRR!!!

Came a mighty roar

That nearly shook the ground

Every animal on the hill

Stopped and looked around.

To the lion's amazement, what they saw

They might not live to tell

They'd never been this afraid before

They all could fight quite well.

Up the hill behind them

Circling for all to see

The biggest, meanest looking dobermans

There could ever be.

Each weighed at least 200 lbs.

All muscle easy to see

Focusing on the lions

Who had no place to flee.

They moved apart, to make a space

Why, only Omar knew

Because through that space

Meanest of them all

Came Nitro and Sai Fon Blue.

They looked around, didn't need no crowns

They were the leaders of Iron Dog Land

Omar turned, to face his pack

Said, "Get ready to meet my clan."

Nitro looked at the lions

Sai Fon looked at her baby boy

If she saw one nick, on Omar's body

She'd command the clan to destroy.

Nitro spoke to the lions

"We know you were looking to fight

So we're gonna make sure

You've had your chance

If we let you leave here tonight."

Omar walked up to them both

"I brought my pack to meet you all

We had put aside the lions

And were really having a ball.

We were about to put an end to this

I planned to do it before you came

Was gonna show those lions, a thing or two

Then send them home in shame".

"We've been watching you" said Nitro

You've quite an amazing pack

We liked the way they stood by you

And had each other's backs.

I know you'd like to finish this

But you all have done enough

We're taking the lions, off your hands

Gonna show them how to be tough.

Omar looked at Booby

He could swear he saw a tear

"Pa let's just send them all back home

We might do this again next year".

All the canines started laughing

Omar's pack and his kin too

Then Sai Fon spoke to the lions

"Tell you what I'm gonna do.

I'll follow my boy's advice this time

But you better get this clear

Omar don't need no watching

But if he needs us

We'll be there.

It was then that Omar Blue looked up

To see his old friend again

Perched in a tree above Sai Fon Blue

Was the giant eagle McZen.

The lions showed a spark of life

Could this really be true

They're not even gonna

Beat us down

Thank you Omar Blue!

Omar's kin opened the circle

But only a little space

For the lions to walk through

One by one

And they looked in each one's face.

Booby and his pride, had gone a ways

Then stopped to take a rest

They wanted to talk about what just happened

Booby told it best.

"I've never been scared like that before

What made us come up here

Did you see the looks they gave us

When they let us out of there.

They called that place Iron Dog Land

And they all were Omar's kin

No wonder he's so big and bold

Look what he grew up in!

And I have to admit, that Omar's pack

Fit in that place just right

That's the bravest bunch of canines

I ever met until tonight."

LET THE FUN BEGIN

(Chapter 14)

Meanwhile back in Iron Dog Land

They were getting along just fine

The pack was very happy

Omar's kin treated them so kind.

They told his kin about K-9 Town

And how they loved it so

They'd stay with them a few days

But then they'd have to go.

The females went with Sai Fon

And the other females there

They all were very beautiful

But were looking at "their" hair.

(Queen Sai Fon)

"You all have hair so nice and soft

And very shiny too

To keep our coats just like that

What would we have to do?"

The females smiled at each other

Then Bee Bee took the lead

I guess I'm the one to talk to

We'll give you what you need.

I have a space in K-9 Town

I do hair and also feet

You'll notice our nails are different colors

We get colors from berries and beets.

One of Omar's kin spoke up
Please teach me what to do
I want to care for hair and feet
I want to be like you.

That's easy said Ms. Bee Bee
I've taught each female here
While they teach the others, what they know
I'll put you in my care.

I'd like to start with Queen Sai Fon
That's if she doesn't mind
I'd like to show her, what I can do
If she'd be so kind.

Sai Fon beamed at Bee Bee

She thought her beautiful too

She had seen Omar look over

Looking at me, or looking at you?

Ummm.

"Of course I'll be the first to try

Wouldn't have it any other way

When I see my Nitro later on

We'll see what he has to say".

MALES TALES

(Chapter 15)

Nitro was over with the males

Telling stories to Omar's pack

They all were fascinated

They'd remember when they got back.

It was then another sibling

They called him Mighty Thor

Said Baby Bro, we saw something tonight

We've never seen before.

Who were the two elders minding the pups

We first thought them too old

We hear they're called the Seers

Quite a name to hold.

We admit our doubts were soon withdrawn

After seeing them in action tonight

Those two females could've handled those lions

They were looking for a fight.

We were watching the females

Herd the puppies

When the Seers said they could go.

Then when one of them

Put the whole through the tree

That convinced them

Not to say no.

When you went towards the battle

They were jumping up and down

We noticed their feet, stayed in the air

And never hit the ground.

All the males started laughing

Even Nitro Blue

He was happy to have his Omar home

And knew Sai Fon was too.

He liked Omar's pack very much

They all loved Omar too

They had as much heart as lions

That much he'd seen was true.

THE SEERS REPENT

(Chapter 16)

We'll ask our Seers over here

They are watching us right now

I think they want an audience

This time I'll get a vow.

They were walking very slowly

He had seen this walk before

"We're sorry, we need our leader

Omar Blue there's something more.

Tonight we made a potion

This one was very new

But now we can't remember

What it made us do.

We know we watched our puppies
There was little there to do
But we don't remember anything else
That's why we came to you."

Omar looked around the group
They pretended sadness too
Then he said to the Seers
In his kindest voice
"You did what we needed you to".

"Thank you leader Omar!
That's what we wanted to hear
That we protected our pack tonight

At least that much is clear".

They were smiling as they walked away
"We've really had our fill
There is something else that can help us now
We're told it's called a pill."

Omar's kin looked at each other
They all had the same thought
The Seers had met Omar's grandma
Minnie Mor was who they sought.

They explained to his pack, that didn't know
How tight those three would be
By the time the Seers left with them
They'd need watching faithfully.

"And oh yes", said the Seers
To the mighty Nitro Blue
"Don't worry we're watching Omar
We'll keep him safe for you".

As soon as they were out of sight
Omar could hold it in no more
"Those Seers are a handful
But one that we adore."

We've told you of their antics
In addition to what you saw
They're very entertaining
What pack could ask for more."

Jai and Ach were helping out

There were many mouths to feed

They prepared their best meal ever

The pack was proud indeed.

Later they shared recipes

Got some good ones too

They'd try them when they got home

A fine meal would be due.

PUPPY TALES

(Chapter 17)

The puppies found some new friends

Exactly their same size

They told their friends about their trip

With just a bit of disguise.

"We had a plan for mountain lion Booby

He got away again

Maybe when we get back home

He'll break into our den.

We can't go out to find him

We were told we'd better not

But when he comes breaking

Through our door

We'll give him what we've got!"

We built a beautiful clubhouse

When we were coming here

Leader Omar liked it so much

He stayed with us in there.

The Iron Dog pups, not to be outdone

Had to tell a tale or two too

We fought a bear in the woods one day

We did what we had to do!

That bear said, "Puppies come with me

We're gonna run away"

We were circling him, when Nitro came

He's still running from us today.

TIME TO SAY GOODBYE

(Chapter 18)

For the next few days

There was nothing but praise

Between the pack and Omar's kin.

They were having a ball

Puppies and all

As the trip came to its end.

Omar sat with his mom and dad

Nitro and Sai Fon Blue

They were looking out at Iron Dog Land

But watching Omar too.

(King Nitro)

"We know you have to leave son
Though we wish that you would stay
We're proud of the life you're living
But don't like you being away.

We're glad you brought you're pack along
We wanted to see them too
We needed to know they were brave and bold
And would always stand with you.

Sai Fon smiled but gave a look
That Omar knew so well
Those mountain lions
Were mighty lucky
They got to leave and tell.

Omar said to his mom and dad
"Don't you worry about me
I don't know why I had to leave
It was fate that made me flee.

You know that bond between us
Will tell you I'm okay
But I've got to get back
To the home we've built
K-9 Town, USA.

I expect you'll be coming
Down our way
I know you want to see
Why I need to leave my home

And my loving family."

Sai Fon perked up right away

"That's right we've already planned

While the females were doing

Our hair and feet

We decided we'd visit your land."

Nitro looked at Omar

And Omar looked at him

The females had gotten together

That meant a lot to them.

"And tell that rascal Major Diggs

He'd better come see me

I forgave you both a long time ago

For what you did to my Big Oak Tree."

(They laughed out loud)

That night the pack, prepared to leave

With their new friends helping out

They felt like they were family

That's what this trip was about!

They were prouder than they had ever been

They couldn't ask for more

Even Bennie Ba the big white wolf

Had made plans with the mighty Thor.

The females were happiest, of them all

They had sat with Sai Fon Blue

They'd never seen anything like her

The mother of Omar Blue.

And Nitro, King of Iron Dog Land
And Omar's father too
Was the mightiest warrior, they'd ever seen
Just like their Omar Blue.

THE TRIP BACK HOME

(Chapter 19)

They said goodbye the next morning

Sadder than they wanted to be

Because in their hearts, they'd made a place

For Omar's family.

But for now they'd put this out of their heads

Because they had to be aware

Aware of their surroundings

And the dangers that might lurk there.

Great Dane Granny, and Rasta Mama

Were talking mighty low

But all the canines could hear them

This they didn't know.

They were talking about their best friend
Omar's granny Minnie Mor
She'd taught those Seers, a thing or two
About potions they could pour.

"We'll wait until we get back home
To see what the new potions can do
Then we'll only use them
To help Leader Omar Blue.
(A sigh of relief was heard)

The trip home was uneventful
Though they were having their usual fun
Their pace was faster than before

Homesickness had begun.

The night before they made it home

The puppies were lagging back

They stopped at a lake for water

Each puppy ran into a sack.

The Elders laughed at the funny scene

They knew it would be soon

They didn't need the sacks earlier

But they'd been keeping up since noon.

So the females carried the puppies

That included Bee Bee too

Two little puppies were in her sack

Looking out at the view.

The puppies made Bee Bee feel special

As she walked with Omar Blue

The mountains so very beautiful

The others thought so too.

Then it came from nowhere

A wonderful, melodious sound

Coming from the back of the pack

But not one head turned around.

It was Lufa the crooning Bloodhound

His voice so smooth and clear

He was howling a beautiful melody

That each of them could hear.

Lufa could howl you into a trance
And he did that starry night
As the pack moved on to K-9 Town
He howled and everything was alright.

They had planned to take another break
To rest and call it a night
But with Lufa's melodies moving them on
They travelled until home was in sight.

They reached K-9 Town at the break of dawn
And stopped at the Big Oak Tree
All were surprised at what they saw
It was Booby and his family.

Booby walked up head hanging down

With a big grin on his face

"Omar Blue we came to thank you

For letting us leave that place.

And we've been doing some thinking

This is a mighty big land

Why can't we all just live in peace

Sometimes give each other a hand.

We know of some water you haven't found

Where the fish jump up at you

And a little spring that stays hot all winter

Bet your females would like that too."

Omar looked at Rottweiler Brady

Who knew that was his cue

The professor nodded his consent

He'd tell Booby what to do.

"We could have settled it one on one

I told you that same day

But you plotted to hurt our entire pack

And now you want to stay.

You'll have your chance to live in peace

Cause that's our leader's way

But one wrong move from any of you

And you'll become our prey.

You didn't get to see us in action

Thanks to our new kin

We want to show you

What we would have done

So please mess up again."

Omar looked at Pitbull Sammy

"Anything you want to add?"

"You know me, I'm not much on words

But I want them to see me mad."

Omar looked at each of his pack

And each one gave a nod

They'd try to do it Booby's way

If it failed they'd come down hard.

Omar turned to Booby

Well I guess that says it all

Now go so we can start living in peace

But you can feel free to call.

Booby smiled and walked away

Thinking they'd give it a try

No reason why it couldn't work

Omar Blue surely wouldn't lie.

Back at their beloved K-9 Town

As happy as could be

The puppies were already playing

A wonderful sight to see.

Omar Blue's Pack surrounded him

It was Brady of course who spoke

"Omar we want to tell you

This trip sure was no joke.

We couldn't imagine the time we'd have
We couldn't have asked for more
This adventure will last forever
What we did and what we saw.

Leader I speak for all of us
You can see it in each face
Thank you for giving up so much
To be with us in this place.

Omar said with a smile on his face
"There was nothing else I could do
My kin would have come to K-9 Town
If that's what it took to meet you.

And I'd like to say how proud I was

Of each and every one of you

As we stood together against those odds

Like no other pack would do.

This wasn't our last adventure

I promise you that today

But wherever we go, we'll always return

To K-9 Town, USA.

As Omar turned to walk away

He looked into the sky

Where McZen the warrior eagle

Winked a fond goodbye.

Made in the USA
Coppell, TX
28 August 2020

35099954R00061